The Gaskitts . . .

Oh, no!

Oh, dear!

Oh, my!

again!

Library of Congress Cataloging-in-Publication Data

Ahlberg, Allan.
The children who smelled a rat / Allan Ahlberg ;
illustrated by Katharine McEwen. — 1st U.S. ed.
p. cm.
Summary: All the Gaskitts have a bad day when the
baby rolls away in a shopping cart, the twins' teacher acts
peculiar, and a lost bird tries to hypnotize the cat.
ISBN 0-7636-2870-0
[1. Pets—Fiction. 2. Teachers—Fiction. 3. Triplets—Fiction.
4. Humorous stories.] I. McEwen, Katharine, ill. II. Title.
WRR PZ7.A2688Ch 2005
[Fic]—dc22   2004062938

2 4 6 8 10 9 7 5 3 1

Printed in China

This book has been typeset in Stempel Schneidler,
Cafeteria, Tapioca, and Kosmik.
The illustrations were done in watercolor and crayon.

Candlewick Press
2067 Massachusetts Avenue
Cambridge, Massachusetts 02140

visit us at www.candlewick.com

Allan Ahlberg

The Children Who Smelled a Rat

illustrated by

Katharine McEwen

CANDLEWICK PRESS
CAMBRIDGE, MASSACHUSETTS

9   The Face..................... 46

10 In the Dungeon.................. 50

11 Elsewhere 56

12 Digging like Crazy!.............. 60

    12a   Horace the Hero......................... 64

    12b   Tricky Situation No.2..................... 68

13, 14, and 15   The Simplified Version . 70

16 Happy Endings 74

Contents

1   The Package 8

2   Bye-Bye, Baby................... 10

    $2\frac{1}{2}$ "Tweet, Tweet!" 12

    $2\frac{3}{4}$ 10 lb 5 oz 13

3   The Teacher Who Wasn't Herself... 14

4   Little Lost Bird 20

5   Frightening Mrs. Fritter.......... 25

6   Look into My Eyes 34

7   Up and Away 38

8   Beethoven and Spinach 40

    8 and a Bit   Meanwhile..................... 44

Meet the Gaskitts

Mr. Gaskitt
The dad.

Mrs. Gaskitt
The mom
and taxi driver.

Gary Gaskitt
The baby.
Eyes: blue.
Hair: brown.
Weight:
~~7 lb 12 oz~~
~~8 lb 4 oz~~
9 lb 10 oz.

he's growing all the time!

Horace Gaskitt: The cat.
Horace has lots of friends.

Mostly cats!

But not all!

Gus and Gloria Gaskitt
The twins.

Picture Dictionary
(some useful words and phrases)

| package | shovel | sea lion | Crunchy Mice | yummy dessert* | dungeon | flabbergasted |

*Actually, there are no yummy desserts in this story, but we thought you'd like to see one all the same.

Chapter 1
The Package

One winter's day, a forgetful man in a green hat and a great hurry, left his umbrella on a train, his briefcase in a bookstore, his book—which he had just bought—on a park bench, and his very special package in a taxi.

Later on, much later actually, when the man came home again, he left his hat on his head, forgot his supper, and went to bed.*

---

 * Which is the last we'll hear of him!

Meanwhile, on that same day—it was a Friday—

Mrs. Gaskitt *found* a package in her taxi.

And when she picked it up,

the package went . . .

Chapter 2
Bye-Bye, Baby

Mr. Gaskitt was minding the baby.

It was his turn.

And doing the grocery shopping

and opening the trunk

and feeling in his pocket

for the parking-lot ticket

and tying his shoelace

and whistling a little tune

and *looking the other way.*

Meanwhile, little Gary—eyes blue,

hair brown,

weight 10 lb 3 oz—

was . . .

Oh, no!

Oh, dear!

Oh, my!

rolling away.

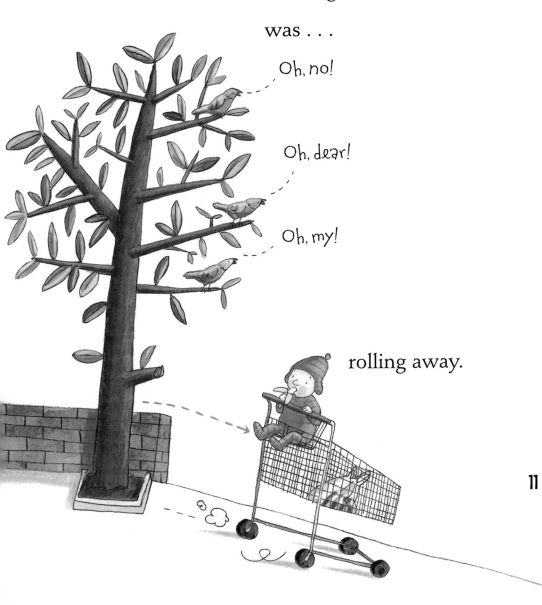

11

Chapter 2 ½ "Tweet, Tweet!"

Horace was at home watching the goldfish when Mrs. Gaskitt came in with the package, unwrapped it, scratched her head, had a cup of tea . . . and went out again.

Tweet, tweet!

Oh, no!

Oh, dear!

Horace watched the package, and the unwrapping.

It was, of course—you guessed, didn't you?—

a little bird in a cage.

A teeny, tiny little bird,

lost and all alone . . .

Tweet!

with a cat.

Chapter 2 ¾ 10 lb 5 oz

Meanwhile, little Gary . . .

was still rolling away.

Oh, my!

Chapter 3
The Teacher
Who Wasn't Herself

So there we are,

a bad day for a little bird,

a bad day for a little baby,

and a bad day, too,

come to think of it,

for Gus and Gloria.

Actually, they had had a bad *week*.

On Monday

their teacher,

Mrs. Fritter, fell off

her bike at the school gates

and had to go home.

And the substitute teacher was . . .

Hands on heads!

Mr. Blotter.

On Tuesday

Mrs. Fritter came back,

tripped over a jump rope,

and went away again.

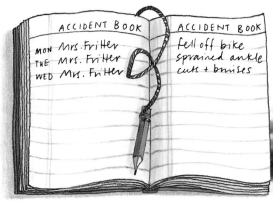

ACCIDENT BOOK

MON Mrs. Fritter
TUE Mrs. Fritter
WED Mrs. Fritter

ACCIDENT BOOK

fell off bike
sprained ankle
cuts + bruises

And the substitute teacher was . .

Ooer!

Mr. Cruncher.

On Wednesday and Thursday

Mrs. Fritter was

run over by a lady

with a stroller . . .

and trodden on

in the doctor's

waiting room.

And the substitute teacher was . . .

Alas, alack!

Mrs. Doom.

17

Now it was Friday, and Mrs. Fritter,

with her arm in a sling, was back again . . .

well, sort of.

But the children were puzzled.

Mrs. Fritter had a funny look in her eye.

She seemed to have forgotten

where things were kept,

and—worse still—

Where's the chalk,
Thingy? - -

ALL THEIR NAMES.

Chapter 4
Little Lost Bird

Horace was back at the house, watching the bird. "A bird," he thought. "A teeny,

tiny little bird, lost and all alone."

And he thought,

"Cats eat birds . . . hmm."

The bird was watching Horace.

She fluffed her feathers,

flicked her tail, opened

her teeny, tiny beak,

and spoke.

"Come here," said the bird.

"Er . . . right," said Horace.

"Look into my eyes," said the bird.

"Right," said Horace.

"Do as I say," said the bird.

"Why should I?" said Horace.

"Do as I say!"

"Er . . . right," said Horace.

Meanwhile, one teeny, tiny baby,

getting bigger though, 10 lb 6 oz,

was—do you remember?—

still rolling away.

Still in the shopping cart

but now on the back of a

truck—did you see that?—

and being chased

by his dad.

Mr. Gaskitt was

running

hard.

Actually, if he'd only known it,
he could have caught a taxi.

Mrs. Gaskitt, at that very moment,
was driving by.

But Mrs. Gaskitt never saw him,
or the baby.
She was watching the car in front,
sucking a peppermint,
thinking of getting her hair cut,
puzzling over that little bird,
and *looking the other way.*

Meanwhile, back at the house . . .

BIRDSEED!

said the bird.

Chapter 5
Frightening Mrs. Fritter

Gus and Gloria's class liked Mrs. Fritter.

She was the kindest,

SILENCE, THINGY!

friendliest,

THINGIES, SIT STILL!

and most popular

STOP THAT, THINGY!

teacher in the whole school.

Well . . . usually.

But today, as you can see and *hear*—

LOST YOUR BOOK? MONSTROUS!

things (and thingies) were different.

Mrs. Fritter frightened
everybody.
She frightened Randolph,
the class rat, who hid in his cage,

and Mr. Blagg,

the principal,

who hid in his office.

When

Mr. Cruncher

came back

for his dumbbells,

she even frightened him.

The children whispered
and passed little notes
to each other . . .

and smelled a rat.
Actually, they really did smell a rat.
Mrs. Fritter wouldn't let them
clean Randolph's cage.
They smelled a couple of
gerbils too, and a hamster.

At play time,

Mrs. Fritter went to the staff room

and . . .

MORE TEA,
MR. THINGY?

frightened the teachers.

Mr. Blagg sneaked in, grabbed a cup of coffee

and a Kit Kat, and sneaked out again.

Back in the classroom, Randolph

crept out for a cookie.

Out in the playground,

Gus, Gloria, and the others

frowned and scratched their heads,

racked their little brains,

and ran around . . .

and *shouted*.

"What's going on?"

"Stop shovin' . . . Thingy!"

"It's a puzzle to me!"

"And me!"

"And me!"

"Shoot, shoot!"

"I think—"*

"My name's not Thingy!"

"It's a mystery to me!"

"She's a changed woman!"

"My theory is—"*

"Who wants a Prott?"

"It's a conundrum!"

"Foul, foul!"

"If you ask me—"*

"Goal!"

"An *enigma*."

"Thingy."

* More later (p. 53)

Meanwhile, Mrs. Fritter stood

staring out the staff-room window.

Spots of rain had begun to fall.

Mrs. Fritter . . . yes.

She was a changed woman, all right:

Longer Hair

A Perfectly good
arm in a sling

Different perfume

Non- existent
cuts and bruises

The rain was streaking the glass.

The face behind it seemed to waver

and dissolve . . .

and *shift its shape.*

Ooer!

Chapter 6
Look into My Eyes

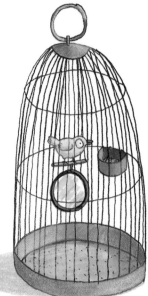

Back at the house—

no birdseed to be found—

the bird was pecking grumpily

at a little bowl of Crunchy Mice.

"They make Crunchy Canaries as well,"

said Horace.

"No, they don't," said the bird.

Later on, the bird began

to complain about her cage.

"It's rubbish, this cage,"

she tweeted.

"Too small—too drafty,

and it needs a good cleaning."

Horace, meanwhile, had crouched down

on his tummy

and was creeping out of the room.

"Come here," said the bird.

And she said, "Open this cage."

"No!" said Horace.

"You'll escape!

You'll get lost!

I'll get into trouble!

I'll . . ."

"Look into my eyes," said the bird.

So anyway,

the bird sat in the window, looking out

at the traffic, while Horace cleaned the cage.

"Put clean newspaper on the floor," said the bird.

"Fill the water bottle. Polish the mirror."

Horace had mixed feelings.

He disliked being bossed around

by a little bundle of feathers.

On the other hand (or paw),

the truth is, he admired the bird.

(And the goldfish,

by the way,

admired him.)

"This bird is cleverer than Randolph,"

thought Horace.

(Horace had met Randolph in an earlier story.)*

And he thought, "I could learn a thing or two."

The bird, meanwhile,

was gazing back into the room.

She fluttered down, perched on Horace's head,

and tweeted in his ear.

Phone for a pizza!

37

*THE CAT WHO GOT CARRIED AWAY: Candlewick Press, $15.99

"Grand and gripping" – THE DAILY VET

"Worth every penny!" – Allan Ahlberg

Chapter 7
Up and Away

Oh, no!

Meanwhile, little Gary Gaskitt—

remember him?—

was *still* rolling away.

Well, up and away really.

Look what's happened

since we saw him last.

This is ridiculous, isn't it?

Whoever saw such a thing?

As fast as Gary is gaining weight —

10 lb 8 oz now!—

his poor old father

is losing it.

Puff, puff!

Oh, dear!

Oh, my!

That crane driver's no help either.

You'd think he'd notice

what's going on.

Instead of which, as you can see,

he's eating a sandwich,

listening to the radio,

waving to his girlfriend

on a passing bus,

rubbing his nose,

scratching his ear,

and *looking the other way*.

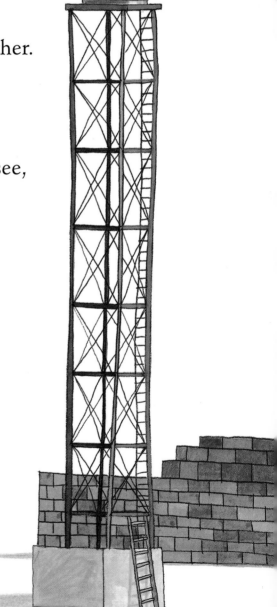

Chapter 8
Beethoven and Spinach

Back in the classroom,

things were going from bad to worse.

Mrs. Fritter lost her temper

over the slightest thing:

a speck of dust

a dropped pin

even . . . breathing.

MONSTROUS!

SILENCE!

THINGY!

Her comments were contradictory

Pay attention!

Who YOU looking at?

or sometimes just plain crazy.

You are absolutely soaking WET!

Gus, Gloria, and the others

could not tell

if they were coming or going.

In the afternoon, for their music lesson

all they heard was Bach, Beethoven, and Brahms.

And in home economics,

all they cooked was spinach pie.

At the end of the day,

Mr. Blagg poked his head

around the classroom door,

flinched, and disappeared again.

Randolph stayed out of sight altogether.

He smelled a rat too.

Till, at last—Yippee!—time to go home.

Mrs. Fritter, with a huge umbrella

in her hand

and a wild look in her eye,

charged out of the classroom,

across the playground,

through the school gates . . .

and away.

SCHOOL

Chapter 8 and a Bit

Meanwhile

I can't phone for a pizza—
I'm a cat!

Yes, you can.

No, I can't!

Yes, you can.

No, I can't!

Look into my eyes....

Yes, I can.

Chapter 9
The Face

It was a wet and gloomy afternoon.

Streetlights were beginning to shine.

Cars had their headlights on.

A little gang of boys and girls came dodging

and weaving along, in and out of shop doorways,

PATISSERIE

PO

POST
MAIL

hiding behind wide ladies and phone booths,

on the trail of a huge umbrella.

There were Gus and Gloria, of course (it's *their* book),

Molly and Tracey and Tom,

Rupert, Eric, and Esmeralda.

Mrs. Fritter marched down High Street

in a straight line.

ICE

BARBER

CAFÉ FRANZ

Large men and fierce-looking dogs

leaped out of her way.

Sensitive infants caught sight

of her wild gaze and burst into tears.

Gus, Gloria, and the others stuck to the trail.

A left turn here. A right turn there.

A gate—a gravel path—a house.

The house was tall and dark.

Mrs. Fritter climbed the front steps

and switched on the porch light.

The children, in the shrubbery,

crouched and watched.

They saw her open the door and step inside.

They saw her in the doorway,
looking back into the street.
And they saw—
they really did—
at the very same time,
her *face,* all watery
and wavering
behind the glass—
one floor below!—
at the basement
window.

Phew!

Chapter 10
In the Dungeon

Yes, phew!

Mrs. Fritter's body

in the doorway.

Mrs. Fritter's face at the window.

The children were astounded, astonished,

and—what's the word?—*flabbergasted*.

Well, no sooner had the front door

closed on Mrs. Fritter No. 1, than down

the basement steps they scrambled

to peer in through the barred

and dusty window at Mrs. Fritter No. 2.

She was sitting on the floor with a broken chair

beside her and a hopeful look in her eye.

The door was locked,

but Gloria found a key under the mat.

Once inside, the children took one look:

broken chair, fallen teacher—

sniffed one sniff: familiar perfume—

and guessed it all.

Of course, this was

the *real* Mrs. Fritter.

The other one,

the crazy imposter,

was . . .

8 : 30 A.M.

No marmalade?
MONSTROUS!

"My *sister*, boys and girls,
here on a visit."
Mrs. Fritter brushed a
cobweb from her hair.
"Gets in funny moods
sometimes."
"Not that funny, Miss!"

"Anyway, she was a bit upset this morning,
and sort of tied me up
and locked me in down here.
I've only just gotten loose."

52

Well, the children were astounded

all over again,

astonished,

and—what's the word?—*affronted.*

"She's not your sister, Miss!" they cried.

"That's right!"

"No way!"

"She's your . . .

EVIL
TWIN!*

53

*Which was actually what Gus had been trying to say back there (p. 31) in the playground. Fancy that!

Then,

just when things were going well,

and the rain had stopped,

and the sky was clear,

and a little bird (no, not that one)

was singing sweetly in the garden,

and the children were congratulating

themselves on a puzzle,

a *conundrum,* solved . . .

a shadowy figure

came down the basement steps

and slammed the door—

and locked it.

Chapter 11
Elsewhere . . .

this was happening:

1. Horace

Horace had sneaked out of the room

while the bird was looking the other way.

He was halfway

> to his friend's house,

>> taking a shortcut

>>> through somebody's garden,

>>> and was at that very moment,

>> only two doors away from

>>> *Mrs. Fritter's* house — Hmm . . .

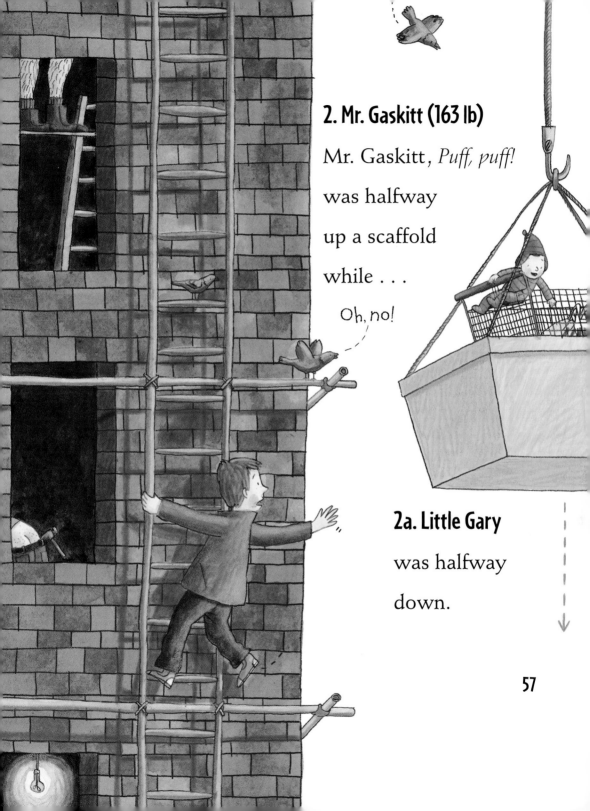

2. Mr. Gaskitt (163 lb)

Mr. Gaskitt, *Puff, puff!* was halfway up a scaffold while . . .

Oh, no!

2a. Little Gary

was halfway down.

3. The Bird

The bird was taking a bath

and singing sweetly.

She loves you,
tweet, tweet, tweet!

Horace, under orders, had found the bathtub

and a few other things

in Gus and Gloria's toy box.

The pizza was, for now, forgotten.

4. Mrs. Gaskitt

Mrs. Gaskitt—

haven't seen much of her lately,

have we?—was also rather busy

at that very moment,

with a tattooed lady and a man in a gorilla suit.

More later.

Chapter 12
Digging like Crazy!

Back in the basement, the situation was . . . Tricky!

The doors were locked, the windows barred.

The children's cell phones were lost,

or left at home, or not charged up.

Their shouts—screams even—

would never be heard on the faraway street.

And Mrs. Fritter's evil twin

was out in the garden . . . with a shovel.

"Fond of gardening, she is," said Mrs. Fritter.

But Gloria (on the table) saw things differently.

Then Gus and the others began to protest.

They wanted a look, got it . . .

and wished they hadn't.

Chapter 12a **Horace the Hero**

Now, the basement door was heavy and thick,

with great big hinges,

a massive lock . . . and a cat flap.

A cat flap. Hmm.

Too small to escape through, of course.

Unless, that is, you were a . . .

Horace, at that very moment,

was making his way

along the garden wall to his friend's house.

And Horace was a cat, wasn't he?

He could do it.

Yes! Yippee! Hooray!

In through the cat flap.

Take a message in his collar.

(If he had a collar.)

Yes, Horace to the rescue!

Horace the Hero!

He would love it,

wouldn't he?

Only trouble was,

Horace never saw the faces at the window

or heard the faint shouts from the house.

He was watching his step

on the slippery wall

(and that scary woman with the shovel),

puzzling over the bossy bird,

thinking of all the things

he would tell his friend . . .

and *looking the other way.*

Chapter 12b Tricky Situation No. 2

As for little Gary—

that teeny, tiny baby,

that brave little bundle—

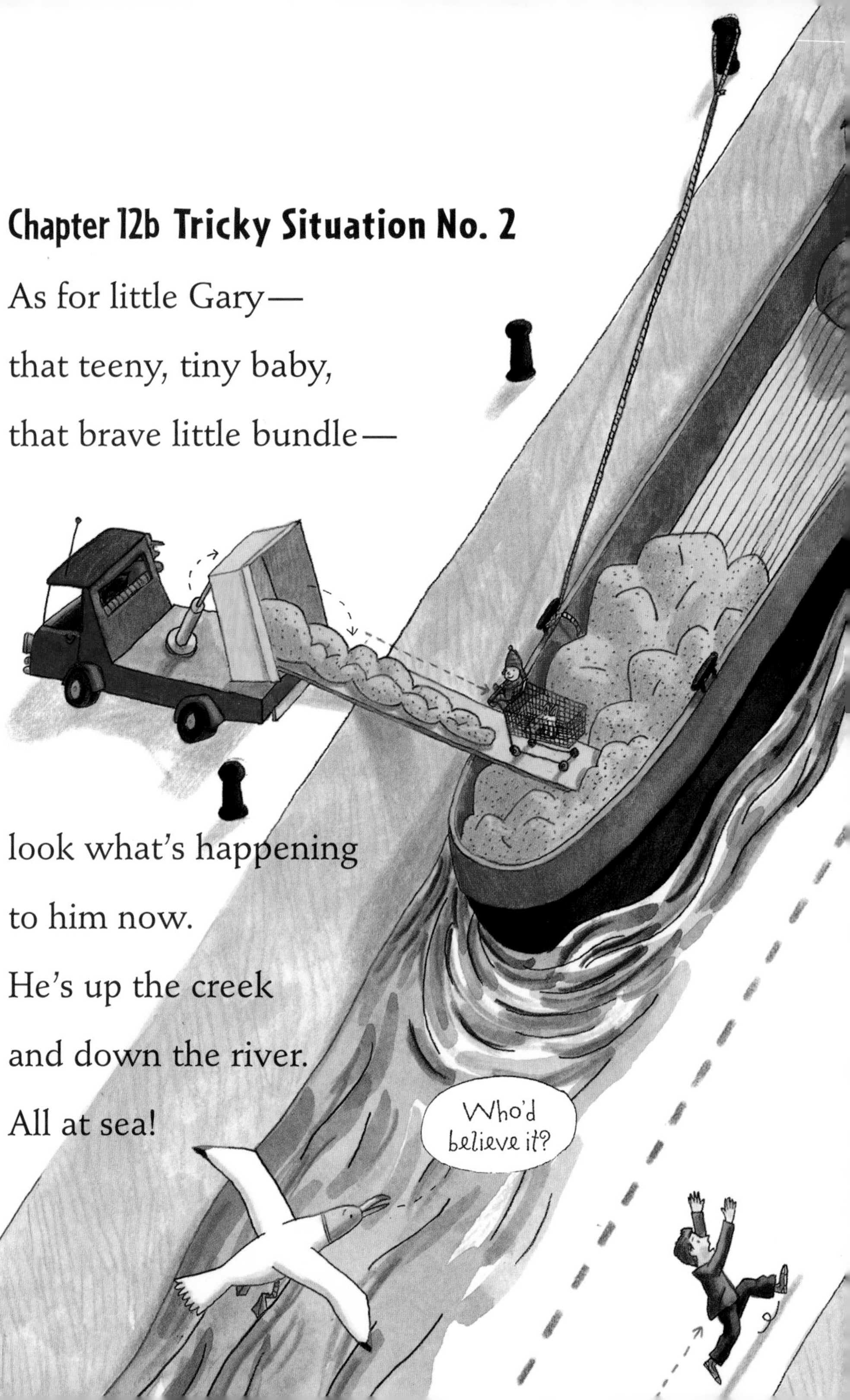

look what's happening

to him now.

He's up the creek

and down the river.

All at sea!

Who'd believe it?

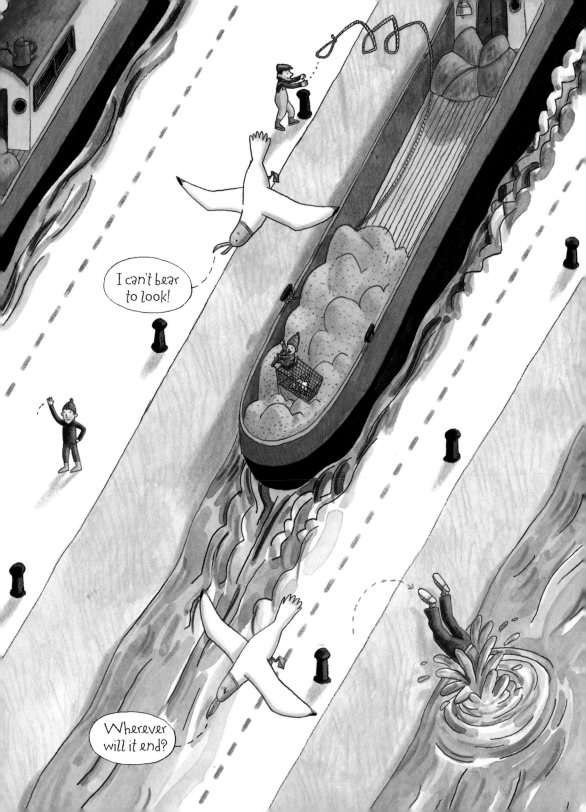

Chapter 13, 14, and 15
The Simplified Version

Look into my eyes!

Meanwhile—Oh, dear, tricky situation No. 3—we're running out of space. Only a few pages left and loads of words still to write. We'll have to squashtheminabit.

Or make 'em smaller. Can you read this at the back? This is too small, isn't it? And this is absolutely ridiculous. How about this? Better? Are you sure? Right—off we go.

So here we are. Back in the basement, Gus, Gloria, and the others were scratching their heads and puzzling over how to escape. Out in the garden, Mrs. Fritter's evil twin had almost disappeared. The hole was deep and getting deeper. The sky was dark and getting darker. Rain was falling again . . . and Horace had given up on visiting his friend and was hurrying home. The bird, meanwhile, was fooling around with a mirror in her little cage, and feeling lonely. Tweet, tweet! Meanwhile also, Mrs. Gaskitt was having a tricky situation of her own with a sea lion and a man on stilts. Something to do with a circus. But that's another story. We'll have to skip it. This is the simplified version.*

Anyway—Puff, puff!—let's keep moving. There's thunder and lightning now. Mrs. Fritter No. 2 is banging around in the tool shed. What's she up to? What's going on? Look out, here she

Smash the door down!

Dig a tunnel!

*Mrs. Gaskitt does have her own story, though, in case you're interested:
THE WOMAN WHO WON THINGS: Candlewick Press, $14.99.
"Unputdownable!" – Allan Ahlberg's mother
"Worth a knighthood." – Queen of England

comes! Meanwhile, Horace is climbing in through his own cat flap, the little bird is reading the paper, and Mr. Gaskitt is . . . swimming? Well Mrs. Fritter No. 2 is almost swimming.

There's a torrent of rain out there . . . and—yes, here she comes—lit up in the lightning flashes—closer and closer—down the steps—the children can see her!—with a key in one hand . . . Mrs. Gaskitt's taxi, by the way, has broken down and a great big hairy man is fixing it. Where were we? Yes, a key in one hand—CRASH! BANG!—and—Oh, no! Oh, dear! Oh, my!—an ax in the other.

An ax. An AX! Oops. Sorry about that. "She looks a bit upset to me," said Mrs. Fritter. The children—Gus and Gloria; Molly and Tracey and Tom; Rupert, Eric, and Esmeralda—agreed.

"She's got an ax, Miss!" they cried.

"She's got a *key*."

"Oh, mother . . ."

"She'll catch her death of cold out there," said Mrs. Fritter. And now the key is in the lock! The door is swinging open! The End is near! Too near, actually. No room for pictures now—no space at all. *Not even for a teeny, tiny frog?* No, Hoppit. Where were we? The End—yes. There she stands in the doorway, Mrs. Fritter's evil twin, with a mad look in her eyes and an ax in her hand. Whereupon—who'd believe it?—another lady comes marching down the steps, opens her mouth, and,

"MARIGOLD, COME HERE!

PUT DOWN THAT AX!

DON'T ARGUE!

LOOK INTO MY EYES!"

The children were amazed, of course, flabbergasted, it goes without saying, and delighted. Mrs. Fritter seemed pleased too. "Chloe!" she cried. "What a pleasant surprise." And then the penny dropped. Oh, dear—no room to swing a cat even. We'll really have to squeeze this in. Sorry. MIAOW?

Anyway, yes, the children took one look at this *familiar* lady No. 3 . . .

and guessed it all.

Chapter 16
Happy Endings

1. The Bird and Horace

When Horace came home and found that teeny,
tiny bird (lost and all alone) *reading the paper,*
he admired her even more.

"Wish I were clever," he said.

"Wish I could read."

"No problemo," said the bird.

She fluttered up and perched on Horace's head.

"I'll teach you."

c.a.t.   Yippee!

I can read!

Now I'm gonna learn ... French!

A B C

2. Mr. Gaskitt and the Baby

Meanwhile, in a café

down by the docks,

little Gary Gaskitt—hair damp,

eyes shut,

weight 10 lb 3½ oz*—

was safe and sound.

So were the groceries.

Mr. Gaskitt was safe

and sound too, and

soaking wet, of course.

And sleepy.

Sweet dreams,

Mr. Gaskitt!

*Yes 4½ oz lighter, i.e., minus one diaper – Poo!

3. Mrs. Fritter and the Children

Back in the basement,

Mrs. Fritter No. 2 had apologized

to Mrs. Fritter No. 1.

Mrs. Fritter No. 3 had given

Mrs. Fritter No. 1 a powerful hug

and taken Mrs. Fritter No. 2

home in her car.

Of course, their names

weren't *all* Mrs. Fritter.

That would be silly, wouldn't it?

No. 2 was Mrs. Trotter,

and No. 3 was Mrs. Molotovski.

So that sorts that out.

Meanwhile *now*, Mrs. Fritter—

minus her alarming sisters—

is upstairs in the kitchen with Gus and Gloria,

Molly and Tracey and Tom,

Rupert, Eric, and Esmeralda,

eating *yummy desserts*.

There wasn't supposed to *be* any yummy

dessert—remember?—but never mind.

This *is* the happy ending after all.

Oh, yes, and finally . . .

4. Mrs. Gaskitt and . . .

Meanwhile also,

Mrs. Gaskitt had said goodbye to the circus

and was back in her taxi.

When she arrived home,

she found a *package* on the back seat.

And when she picked it up—

Oh, no!

Oh, dear!

Oh, my!—

the package went . . .

Oink!*

*Fancy that.